W9-BXX-664

STERLING CHILDREN'S BOOKS
New York

STERLING CHILDREN'S BOOKS
New York

An Imprint of Sterling Publishing Co., Inc.
1166 Avenue of the Americas
New York, NY 10036

STERLING CHILDREN'S BOOKS and the distinctive Sterling Children's Books logo
are registered trademarks of Sterling Publishing Co., Inc.

Text © 2020 Katie Tsang and Kevin Tsang
Illustrations © 2020 Nathan Reed
Additional illustrations © 2020 Egmont Ltd.

All rights reserved. No part of this publication may be reproduced,
stored in a retrieval system, or transmitted in any form or by any means
(including electronic, mechanical, photocopying, recording, or otherwise)
without prior written permission from the publisher.

ISBN 978-1-4549-3736-4

Distributed in Canada by Sterling Publishing co., Inc.
c/o Canadian Manda Group, 664 Annette Street
Toronto, Ontario, M6S 2C8, Canada

For information about custom editions, special sales, and premium and corporate purchases,
please contact Sterling Special Sales at 800-805-5489 or specialsales@sterlingpublishing.com.

Manufactured in China
Lot #:
2 4 6 8 10 9 7 5 3 1
11/19

sterlingpublishing.com

FOR OUR GRANDPARENTS:
MIMI, POP, GRANDPA BOB,
GRANDMA KAY
AND
PO-PO, NA-NA, YE-YE,
GUNG-GUNG

-Katie & Kevin Tsang

CONTENTS

CHAPTER 1

SPIDERS ARE SNEAKY

My name is **Sam Wu,** and I am <u>**NOT**</u> afraid of spiders.

I recently went on a camping trip. You might think camping out in the woods is where I had to face spiders, but no. That was where I had to prove I was <u>**NOT**</u> afraid of the dark.

It is very dark in the woods. And only the **BRAVEST** can survive

spending the night out in the dark. Luckily, I was with my **best friends** Bernard and Zoe, and we came up with a plan. Less luckily, I was also there with my cousin Stanley, who is kind of a know-it-all, and Ralph, who is my nemesis. We've been enemies for a long time. He was the one who first started calling me **Scaredy-Cat Sam**, which forced me to prove to everyone how brave I was.

Anyway, it was a close call, but we survived the dark. And I know part of the reason was because I kept thinking what **Spaceman Jack**

2

and **Captain Jane** would do![1] Whenever I'm in a tough situation, I imagine them right there with me.

And, before the dark, I had to face sharks *and* ghosts! I'm now

an experienced shark evader, certified ghost hunter, and on top of all of that, I'm a seasoned snake wrangler. Even **Spaceman Jack** is afraid of snakes!

---

[1] **Spaceman Jack** and **Captain Jane** are the main characters on SPACE BLASTERS, which is the best show in the whole universe! They have lots of adventures, and I want to be just like them. Ralph says he thinks the show sounds stupid, but he doesn't know what he's talking about.

I thought that after everything that had happened, with surviving the dark, that things would feel different at school, but life continued as normal.

I was still best friends with Zoe and Bernard. My cousin Stanley went back to

Hong Kong, and I actually **missed** him. Even though he's a know-it-all, he can be kind of useful sometimes.

And Ralph was still my nemesis. I thought maybe he'd be nicer after we survived the dark together and **solved the mystery** of what had been creeping around our campsite, but I was wrong. He still called me Sam Wu-ser and

made fun of **SPACE BLASTERS**.
We were definitely <u>**NOT**</u>
friends.

Ralph's twin sister,
Regina, who had been
camping with us, was still
nice. Even nicer in fact.

My little sister, Lucy, was still
the **actual** bravest person I knew, and her
cat, Butterbutt, was usually
to blame for
most things.
I thought
that my time
of **facing my
fears** was
behind me.

After all, I'd already faced ghosts, sharks, and the dark.

But then came the **SPIDERS!**

After everything, I thought I'd be prepared. Because here's the thing about spiders. They're sneaky. They can get you when you least expect them. And before you know it—**BAM**—they have you in their web.

It would be up to me to save everyone. Just like **Spaceman Jack** would do.

CHAPTER 2

TULIP THE TARANTULA

To be honest, I'd never thought that much about spiders before.

I'd seen them, of course, making webs in the garden or in a corner of the kitchen but they'd always been small. And I didn't like the feeling of walking into a spiderweb, feeling its **sticky strands** getting caught on me, almost like getting a hug from a ghost. But, really, it was easy to brush the web away and carry on with my adventures.

My friend Bernard, however, had thought a **LOT** about spiders.

Bernard is the smartest kid in our whole grade, and **he loves facts**. Every day, he tells us a new fact about something. Some are more interesting than others.

On this day, they were all about spiders. "Did you know," he said as he put on his glasses[2],  "the silk in a spider's web is **five times** stronger than a strand of steel? Or that there are almost forty thousand

---

[2] Bernard doesn't actually need glasses, but he likes to put on a pair of "thinking" glasses before he says something smart, which is at least three times a day.

different types of spiders?"

Zoe shuddered and ran her hands through her hair like she was looking for **tiny spiders**.

"Or did you know that they don't use muscles in their legs, but move using hydraulic pressure? Like **ROBOTS**!"

"I did not know that," I admitted. "Why have you been researching so much about spiders?"

"Don't you remember?" Bernard replied. "Today the sixth graders are coming to our class to show us the **tarantula** that lives in their science lab."

I frowned. I'd heard of tarantulas, but I couldn't one hundred percent remember what they were.

Bernard sensed my confusion. "Big, hairy spiders," he said, his eyes huge. "I've never seen one in real life, just in pictures."

I swallowed. "**No big deal**," I said, even though my heart was starting to beat very fast. "I bet Fang could beat a tarantula in a battle. He'd probably eat it for breakfast."

Fang is my **VERY** fierce, **VERY** dangerous pet snake. He's my sidekick, and only the bravest people in the world, like me, can handle him. I got him at the pet store a while back to prove how brave I was.

My little sister, Lucy, thinks she can hold him, but she doesn't understand how **ferocious** he is, even though I've told her a million times. She thinks he's cute. Which is ridiculous!

"I don't know," Bernard said,

shaking his head. "Fang is pretty **ferocious**, but I think tarantulas can take down prey over twice their size. And they actually *do* have fangs."

Bernard says Fang is misnamed because he *technically* doesn't have fangs, but I think the name suits him perfectly.

I swallowed again. I didn't like the idea of coming face-to-face with ***anything*** that had fangs.

"I like spiders," Regina chimed in, pushing her hair out of her eyes. "Do you think they'll let us hold it?"

"**Probably not**," I said quickly. "Just for everyone's safety." I turned to Bernard. "Right, Bernard?"

He shrugged. "I don't know," he said. "They're sixth graders. Who knows what they'll do."

Word spread quickly about the spider and the sixth graders coming to our class. Our teacher, Ms. Winkleworth, had to put four names on the Not Listening Board and clap her hands **six times** before we settled down.

Luckily, my name wasn't on the board. Neither was Zoe's or Bernard's or Regina's. Or Ralph's—but that **wasn't lucky**. I wouldn't

13

have minded seeing his name up there.

"Now, class," said Ms. Winkleworth, "we're going to be on our very **best behavior** for our sixth grade visitors, correct?"

"Yes, Ms. Winkleworth," we all chorused back.

"And we'll stay in our seats and only talk when we're called on, correct?"

"Yes, Ms. Winkleworth."

"Very good," she said. "I don't want to put anyone else's name on the board."

We all sat in silence. My heart was beating **very fast** inside my chest, but that was because I was ready for anything. I used to think this feeling meant I was nervous, but now I know it is the feeling I get when I need to be extra brave.

The door opened and
four sixth graders walked
in with their science teacher,
Mr. Dougal.

And he was holding a

HUGE

spider.

In his hands!

15

CHAPTER 3

SPIDERS ARE NOT FOR SNUGGLING

The entire class took in a deep breath as one, like we suddenly all shared a gigantic lung. Mr. Dougal walked to the front of the class and then he **PUT THE SPIDER DOWN ON THE TABLE**.

I wanted to back away, but it is almost impossible to do that when you are sitting in a chair that is attached to your desk. So instead, I just leaned back as far as I could.

"This is Tulip," Mr. Dougal said affectionately, stroking the back of the **GIANT** spider as if it were a kitten. The spider was practically the size of a kitten, so it was easy for him to pet it. "Tulip is a Goliath birdeater tarantula."

"It eats *birds*?" Zoe said, her eyes huge.

"Zoe, don't call out without raising your hand," said Ms. Winkleworth, but she was staring at the spider with eyes almost as big as Zoe's.

"Great question," Mr. Dougal replied. "**Goliath birdeater tarantulas** can, in fact, eat birds, but they usually eat insects."

One of the sixth graders stepped forward. "But they sometimes eat other animals like **RATS** or even **SNAKES**."

SNAKES? I thought of Fang. In a fight between Tulip and Fang, I wasn't sure who would win. I gulped. I never thought I'd come across an animal fiercer than Fang.

Another one of the sixth graders spoke up. "Goliath birdeater tarantulas are the biggest spiders in the world. This one is an average size."

AN AVERAGE SIZE?

The spider was bigger than my hand! Maybe even bigger than my face! **NOT** that I was going to get close enough to compare the size of my face to the size of the spider. Even just thinking about having my face near it made my palms **a little** sweaty.

Mr. Dougal carefully picked the tarantula up

again and held it out for us to see. It was light brown with black patterns on it.

"Any other questions, class?" said Ms. Winkleworth, who was standing **very close** to the door.

I raised my hand. "I thought spiders had eight legs," I said. This was something everyone knew. "But it looks like this one has . . ." I paused and counted. "Ten! Or even twelve!"

"Very observant," said Mr. Dougal. "As you can see, she has eight legs as well as what *looks* like two other sets." He used his other hand to point at what I'd thought was another pair of legs and explained, "These are called pedipalps—they're like pincers. Scorpions also have them."

Despite my best efforts to stay **very still**,

I shuddered.

"And these," he said, pointing at the things closest to the tarantula's face, "are the chelicerae[3], which are similar to jaws."

"Her jaws are **OUTSIDE** her mouth?" I asked. I was so overwhelmed by this information, I forgot to raise my hand. Ms. Winkleworth gave a warning cough.

"They aren't exactly jaws, just similar to jaws. They are connected to the venom gland," Mr. Dougal went on, like this was a perfectly normal, **not-at-all-terrifying** thing. Then he smiled

I was NOT scared at all!

---

[3] He pronounced this like "kuh-lis-er-uh," which sounded like it could be a type of alien on **SPACE BLASTERS**.

at us. "Does anyone know what venom is?"

Bernard's hand shot up into the air.

"Yes?"

"Venom is a kind of poison that animals can use to protect themselves."

"**Precisely!**" said Mr. Dougal. "But don't worry—tarantulas very rarely bite humans. And if you are unlucky enough to get bitten, the venom isn't any more dangerous than a wasp sting."

"Has Tulip ever bitten anyone?" I asked.

"Sam," said Ms. Winkleworth, "if you speak out **one more time** without raising your hand, I'm going to have to put your name on the board."

"Not in all the time I've known her," said Mr. Dougal, stroking the back of the giant spider again. It was **impossible** to see if Tulip was enjoying being petted. She didn't purr like a cat or anything. She just sat there, staring at us with her eight eyes.

!!! EIGHT EYES !!!

EIGHT!

I started to ask another question, but then remembered what Ms. Winkleworth had said and put my hand up in the air.

"Yes?" said Mr. Dougal, smiling at me.

"How long have you known Tulip?" I asked. This was very important. If Mr. Dougal had only known Tulip for a little while, who knew if she could be **trusted?**

"I've known Tulip her whole life," said Mr. Dougal. "She's four now, and will hopefully live for **many** years to come."

Regina put her hand in the air. "Can I hold her?" she asked.

My mouth dropped open.

"I'm afraid not," said Mr. Dougal. "I have years of experience holding tarantulas, but ones like Tulip can occasionally get aggressive, and so it isn't a good idea for someone inexperienced to hold her."

Aggressive? What did he mean, Tulip

could get aggressive? Why had he brought an **AGGRESSIVE GIANT SPIDER** into our classroom?

"But you can come up here and pet her, if you are **VERY** gentle," said Mr. Dougal.

Regina hopped up and went straight to the tarantula. I couldn't believe it!

She very gently ran one finger down the top of its back and wrinkled her nose. "She's so **furry!**" she exclaimed. "Almost like a hamster or something. But bristlier!"

"And bigger," I muttered.

"Hi, Tulip," Regina cooed at the spider. "Do you want to snuggle?"

"Of course she doesn't want to **snuggle!**" I burst out. "She's a spider!"

Suddenly, the spider turned
toward Regina, lifted up on her hind
legs, and bared her **HUGE** fangs at her!
Regina took a step back.

I was almost one hundred percent certain that Tulip was going to **pounce**, but she just stayed in Mr. Dougal's hands with her front legs up in the air and her fangs out for everyone to see.

"Oh, settle down there, Tulip," said Mr. Dougal, stepping away from the desk. He turned to one of the sixth graders, who was holding a plastic container. "Here, let's put Tulip back in her carrying case." He slid Tulip into the case, where she landed with a **thump** and then scurried around.

Just to be safe, I shut my eyes. I wished I was wearing one of the helmets they wear on **SPACE BLASTERS**. Or even better, a whole **SPACE BLASTERS** protective suit!

"Nothing to worry about!" said Mr. Dougal
in that fake-cheerful voice adults use when
there is **DEFINITELY** something to worry
about. "Just stay calm! Tulip can sense all the
excitement."

"I can sense that Sam Wu-ser is scared of
the spider," sneered Ralph with a snort. "His
eyes are closed! He's too scared to even **look**
at her!"

Ralph was sitting behind me, so I had no

idea how he knew this. I opened my eyes as wide as I could and turned around to face Ralph. "**Am not**," I said. "I was just blinking!" I did a few slow blinks to emphasize this fact.

Ralph Philip Zinkerman the Third was **DEFINITELY** still my nemesis.

"Settle down, class," said Ms. Winkleworth. I don't think she heard Ralph teasing me, and I wasn't going to tattle. "This has certainly been exciting," she added, sounding out of breath like she'd just run a marathon, even though she'd only been standing by the door. "Perhaps it's time for you all to go back to the sixth grade classrooms?"

Now that my eyes were open, I could see that Tulip was still scurrying around the container, and she did **<u>NOT</u>** look happy.

Well, she looked about the same as when she had come in, and she hadn't looked happy then either.

"Does anyone have any questions for Mr. Dougal or the sixth graders?" asked Ms. Winkleworth.

At least **fifteen** hands went up in the air. Tulip lifted a leg and tapped it against the side of her container, like she too wanted to ask something.

"Oh dear, that's a lot of questions," said Ms. Winkleworth. Then she brightened. "How about we spend the afternoon discussing what we learned from Mr. Dougal, and then we can write down our questions and send them over later. Does that sound good to you, Mr. Dougal?"

"Excellent plan," said Mr. Dougal. "Now, as you say, we should probably get back to our class. Tulip seems to be uncharacteristically **agitated**—I think she wants to be back in her tank. This is the farthest she's ever traveled!"

I wondered who had thought this would be a good idea.

"What do we say, class?" said Ms. Winkleworth as Mr. Dougal and the four sixth graders made their way to the door.

"Thank you!" we all chorused together, and then the classroom door **slammed** shut behind them.

I thought that would be the last I'd see of Tulip the tarantula.

 I WAS WRONG.

CHAPTER 4

SPIDERS VS. LEOPARDS

After class, it was time for lunch. I grabbed my **SPACE BLASTERS** lunchbox and walked with Zoe and Bernard to the cafeteria. I was especially excited because my mom had packed my **favorite** lunch, char siu bao[4] and egg tart pastries. There were also some

---

[4] Char siu bao are fluffy, white buns stuffed with delicious barbecued pork. My mom makes them for me once a week. They are the BEST.

carrots, but I wasn't as excited about those.

"Did you two **SEE** the size of Tulip's fangs?" asked Bernard as we sat down at our usual table. "They were as long as my fingers!" Bernard wiggled his fingers out in front of him for emphasis.

I **shuddered**. Tulip's fangs *were* about the same size as Bernard's fingers.

"And you could just tell Tulip was ready to pounce," Bernard continued. He looked me right in the eyes. "And before you know it . . .

Bernard lunged at me and dug his fingers into my arm like claws.

"**Ahhh!**" I yelled as I swatted Bernard's hands away.

Bernard gave me a serious look. "Too slow," he said. "You're already spider food."

MUNCH!

Munch!

MUNCH!

I shuddered again. Getting bitten by a spider would be the worst. Especially by a spider that was as big as **my face**. If spiders could eat birds, could they eat people, too?

"Stop scaring Sam," said Zoe, cutting in.

"I'm not scaring Sam!" said Bernard.

"Yeah, plus I'm **NOT** scared!" I said. I paused and looked back at Zoe. "But I mean, *you* would be scared if you were attacked by a *man-eating* spider."

Zoe sighed and tossed a chicken nugget from her plate at Bernard. "Bernard is no man-eating spider."

"True," said Bernard, picking up the discarded chicken nugget from the table and putting it in his mouth. "But just think of those **fangs!**" He wiggled his fingers out in front of him again.

Zoe rolled her eyes.

"Okay, okay, *Spider-Bernard,*" I said, leaning away. "We get it. No more pouncing on anyone at lunch."

Bernard shrugged and continued munching on the chicken nugget.

I couldn't shake the feeling that Tulip the tarantula had been watching me—**specifically me**—back in the

37

classroom. Staring me down. **Sizing me up**.
And I would know from experience, because Fang
stares me down all the time, and also from
this one time at the aquarium with a shark
called Crazy Charlie. I just get a feeling
when a ferocious beast is staring at me
and probably wants to **eat me**.

IT WAS VERY SCARY!

It'd been hard to tell *exactly* where
Tulip had been looking because she had
eight eyes, but I was almost a hundred
percent sure that all **eight** of her
beady eyes had been looking *directly* at
me. I bet if Tulip had had her way, she'd

be having me for lunch right then.

I felt a shiver run down my spine.
I was going to stay as far away
as **possible** from that tarantula.
Even if it meant I had to switch schools
by the time I got to the sixth grade.

"Hey, you guys," said a familiar voice from
behind us.

I looked up. It was Regina, holding a lunch
tray. "How **COOL** was Tulip?" she said, sitting
down next to Zoe.

"Erm," I said, staring at my char siu bao.
"Pretty cool?"

"I'm going to ask my parents if I can get a
giant tarantula," Regina said, cheerfully
munching on a slice of pizza. "But I bet they'll
say no." She lowered her voice.

"It's because Ralph is actually really scared of spiders."

I had a sudden, newfound, begrudging[5] respect for Ralph. I wondered if this was why he'd been so determined to make **ME** look scared of the spider, so nobody would know that *he* was super terrified.

"I didn't know you were so into spiders, Regina," said Bernard, sounding impressed. "Did you know that there are over **forty**

---

[5] "Begrudging" is a word I learned on SPACE BLASTERS. It means when you do something even though you don't want to. Sometimes Captain Jane will begrudgingly let Spaceman Jack drive their spaceship.

thousand types of spiders in the world?"

"Wow," said Regina, suitably excited.

"Sometimes my sister's cat, Butterbutt, eats spiders," I offered. I didn't know any spider facts.

Regina scrunched her face up. "Cats will eat **anything**," she said.

I nodded. She wasn't wrong.

"What are you going to write for your question for Mr. Dougal?" Regina asked. "I have so many questions about Tulip!"

My main question was how I could properly protect myself from a Goliath birdeating tarantula, but I wasn't going to admit that out loud.

"Um, how big their webs get," I said instead.

I actually was a little bit curious about that. A web would have to be **HUGE** to hold a spider that big!

"Oh, that's a good one!" said Regina.

"I want to know how fast they can move," said Zoe. "I'm guessing I can probably outrun one, but it would be good to know **for sure**."

"I want to know what Mr. Dougal feeds her,"

said Bernard. "Does she need to eat live prey, like Fang? Does she eat bugs? Other spiders?"

"What about you, Regina?" I quickly asked, partly to change the subject from what Tulip ate for lunch. I still **wasn't** convinced that she didn't eat humans.

"I want to know what predators they have!"

I thought about how Butterbutt chased spiders in our garden. "Probably **giant cats**," I said. "Especially if they live in the jungle."

I imagined a battle between a leopard and a giant tarantula. Just one leopard could probably eat a giant tarantula, but I bet a whole group of tarantulas could take down a leopard if they worked together.

I shuddered at the thought of an **ARMY** of giant tarantulas. If even a leopard couldn't win against them, I wouldn't stand a chance.

CHAPTER 5

THE GREAT ESCAPE

After lunch, we all wrote down our questions about spiders, specifically about Tulip. Ms. Winkleworth said she'd never seen us so focused. We had a **LOT** of questions.

"Now," she said, when we'd handed in all our questions. "Who would like to go deliver these to Mr. Dougal for me?"

Regina's hand shot up in the air, and then before I had a chance to protest, she **grabbed** mine and raised it, too.

I looked at Regina in horror. But I didn't want anyone to know that I secretly **never** wanted to see Tulip ever again, so I didn't say anything. She grinned at me. "You're the bravest person I know," she said solemnly. "I know you **won't** be scared to see Tulip again, right?"

I gulped. "Right," I said.

"Great, thank you, Regina and Sam," Ms.
Winkleworth said. "The two of you can go. But
come **straight back**, all right?"

I blinked. It looked like I didn't have a
choice. But I wasn't just going to go as a
two-person team. We needed backup. I looked
at Bernard and tried to wink. Sometimes on
SPACE BLASTERS, the alien Five-Eyed Frank will
wink at **Spaceman Jack** or **Captain Jane** to
let them know that he has the situation
under control. This was the opposite of
that—I did **NOT** have the situation under
control at all, but I was hoping that Bernard
would understand what I wanted.

"What's in your eye, Sam?" Regina said,
frowning at me.

I'm not very good at winking.

47

"**Nothing**," I said. Then I cleared my throat and coughed, the way that grown-ups do when they are trying to get someone's attention.

"Are you okay, Sam?" asked Ms. Winkleworth, looking concerned.

"I'm fine," I said, still staring hard at Bernard.

"Oh!" said Bernard. He finally got it. "Can I go, too, Ms. Winkleworth? I'd really like to see Tulip again."

Then Bernard kicked Zoe in the ankle.

"Ow!" yelled Zoe, scowling at Bernard, before she realized what he'd been doing.

"Um, yeah, me too, Ms. Winkleworth!" she said. "I know the way to the sixth grade science lab."

Ms. Winkleworth rubbed between her eyes and sighed.

"I **don't** think this is a four-person job," she said. "At this rate, the whole class will want to go."

"I don't," Ralph said loudly from the back of the classroom. "Who wants to run errands? I'm not a mailman."

His friends around him all laughed.

"Is that right, Ralph Zinkerman?" Ms. Winkleworth replied with an arched eyebrow and a stern look that was maybe even scarier than Tulip's **eight-eyed** one.

Ralph sank down in his seat.

Ms. Winkleworth swung her gaze round on us.

"Off the four of you go. But hurry back."

I still wasn't **especially** eager to go anywhere near Tulip, but I felt better now that I had my friends with me as we all scrambled up from our desks. It was just like when **Spaceman Jack** from SPACE BLASTERS says he can do anything when he's got his crew with him.

It felt strange being in the empty halls while everyone else was in class.

"This is so **exciting!**" said Regina, skipping down the hall ahead of us.

"I can run as fast as I want down the hall, and nobody can stop me!" said Zoe, and then she did exactly that.

"**Wait for us!**" cried Bernard, huffing as he

ran to catch up with the girls.

I was the one carrying the envelope full of questions, so I didn't run in case I dropped it and the slips of paper flew everywhere. Then we'd really be in trouble.

I'd never been to the side of the school where the sixth grade classrooms were. But Zoe knew the way because she had two older brothers **AND** an older sister who had showed her all over the school. She even knew how to get around the high school thanks to her big sister, Mallory.

"The science lab is right around this corner," said Zoe, and we followed her to a blue door that was slightly ajar.

There was **a lot** of noise coming from inside the lab. People were **shouting** and **running**, and it sounded like tables and chairs were being pushed around. The four of us paused and looked at each other. "Sixth grade science sounds pretty exciting," said Regina.

Just then the door burst open, nearly hitting us all in the faces. We jumped back. A red-cheeked sixth grade boy ran out, panting.

He slammed the door behind him.

"TULIP'S ON THE LOOSE!" he shouted. "Did you see where she went?"

"Bobby, get back in here!" yelled a voice from inside. "We don't want to cause a panic!"

If you asked me, this seemed like the **perfect** time to panic. But I just stared open-mouthed at red-faced Bobby.

I WAS NOT SCARED!

"We've . . . er . . . brought some questions for Mr. Dougal?" Regina tried. "Is everything okay in—?"

"What do you mean, Tulip is **on the loose**?" Zoe cut in, asking the question we were all thinking.

"What do you think it means?" exclaimed Bobby. "It means Tulip, who is a tarantula by the way—sorry, I don't know if I made that part clear—has made her great escape."

"Bobby, who are you talking to? I told you, we've got **everything** under control," said the same voice from inside the classroom. Then the door opened and Mr. Dougal slipped out into the hall. "Get back inside the classroom, Bobby."

Bobby scurried back inside as Mr. Dougal

turned to face us. He did **NOT** look like he had everything under control. His hair was sticking up in every direction, his tie was undone, and he was sweating like he'd just run a race.

"Oh, hello there," he said when he saw us. He tried to smile, but it turned into more of a **grimace**.

"I . . . erm . . . forgot that you would be coming by this afternoon. Do you have the questions?"

He took the envelope out of my hands. "Wow, that is a lot! It might take me a while to answer all of these. Especially as I'm a bit . . . busy at the moment. Now, hurry back to your class. Nothing to see here, **nothing at all**," he added as he shepherded us away from the door. As he did, I got a glimpse inside the classroom. Some kids were crawling on their hands and knees, looking under desks and bookshelves. Others were standing on their chairs, **like the floor was made of lava**.

"Sir," said Regina carefully, "has Tulip escaped?"

Mr. Dougal ran his hand through his hair, making it stick up even more. "No, no, I wouldn't say *escaped*. We've just . . . misplaced her. That's it. She's misplaced. I'm sure she's just hiding somewhere **in** the classroom."

I thought of how the door had been a bit open when we'd arrived, and I knew there was a very good chance that Tulip was **NOT** inside the classroom.

"Well, nothing to worry about! Hurry back now," said Mr. Dougal, smiling slightly manically. And then he disappeared back into the science lab with the envelope.

We all looked at each other.

"I **don't** think Mr. Dougal is going to find Tulip," Regina said slowly. "He didn't really seem like he knew what he was doing." She looked up at us. "I think we might have to step in."

I knew then that Regina was right. It was **up to us**. After all, we already were ghost hunters, snake wranglers, shark evaders and explorers of the dark. Who else in the school had that kind of experience? We were the only ones prepared to be spider catchers. It wasn't going to be easy, but as **Spaceman Jack** says, **"If it was easy, everyone would do it. It's the hard things in life that require the most bravery."** And maybe this would be the way I could prove once and for all to Ralph, and to everyone else, that I was **NOT** a scaredy-cat.

I looked solemnly around at my crew. "You're right. It's up to us to find Tulip. We need a plan."

CHAPTER 6

EMERGENCY MEETING

After school, we **ambushed** our parents in the pickup spot by the parking lot and asked if everyone could come over to my house. Usually my mom likes to arrange these things in advance, but it was an emergency.

I told her as much. "Mom," I said. "It's an

EMERGENCY."

"What kind of emergency?" she said skeptically, holding on to Lucy with one hand.

59

"Is it anything I should know about? Or any of the other parents?"

"No, **nothing** like that," I said quickly. "It's a kid emergency. You wouldn't understand."

My mom sighed and looked at Bernard's dad and Zoe's mom. "If it's all right with Bernard's and Zoe's parents," she said, "then it's fine with me. You can stay for dinner."

We all cheered.

Then I remembered Regina. "Mom, there's another friend we wanted to invite as well. Could you ask Regina's parents if she can come over, too?" I pointed at where Regina was standing with her parents and Ralph.

"Sam, you know if we invite Regina, we have to invite her brother, Ralph, too," said my mom.

My mom is a big believer in being **"fair"** and **"welcoming."** I sighed. There was going to be no getting out of it. No matter how much I didn't want to spend any more time with Ralph than I absolutely had to. Part of me wondered if maybe, just maybe, he'd be nicer outside school, like he had been when we'd gone camping. But I doubted it. Like **Spaceman Jack** says, **"An alien leopard doesn't usually change its spots."**

It turned out Ralph and Regina had piano lessons, so they weren't able to come over anyway.

Ralph **couldn't** believe I had invited him and Regina to my house. "Who would want to go to Sam Wu-ser's house?" he sneered under his breath when our parents couldn't hear us.

"You weren't really invited anyway," I muttered. "It was because my mom made me."

"Even if I was, I wouldn't have wanted to come," Ralph shot back.

"Well, I wouldn't have wanted you to come," I said.

"Well, even if you **had** wanted me to come, I wouldn't have wanted to come. The only reason I hung out with you guys while we were camping was because I had **no** other options."

We glared at each other. Ralph was still the worst.

"Have fun at your house with your zombie werewolf," I muttered. Regina had told us that she and Ralph were convinced there was a **zombie werewolf** trapped in their basement. She wanted me, Bernard, and

Zoe to come over to investigate, but so far it hadn't happened. I **wasn't** sure if I was ready to face a zombie werewolf, if I was being totally honest.

The mention of the zombie werewolf worked on Ralph. He went pale and then stormed off after his parents and Regina.

"Come on, Sam!" my mom called from her car. I ran after her and hopped in the car with Zoe, Bernard, and Lucy.

The first thing we did when we got back to my house was stock up on **snacks**. Everyone knows sustenance[6] is the secret to having a

---

[6] "Sustenance" is a fancy way to say "food." **Captain Jane** always calls her food "sustenance." Basically, on **SPACE BLASTERS**, they have their Space Nutrient Packs, and here on Earth, I have jelly beans.

successful planning session.

I grabbed some jelly beans, string cheese, oranges, and crackers, and we went outside to plot. My mom gave us a blanket to spread out on the grass. "For your picnic," she said.

"It's **NOT** a picnic," I said. "It's a very important, **top-secret** planning session."

"Okay, Sam," said my mom with a smile. "Would you like some juice with your important, top-secret planning session?"

"Yes, please, Mrs. Wu!" said Zoe.

I turned to my friends. "Okay," I said seriously. "Let's go over what we know. Bernard, can you write this all down?"

Bernard reached into his backpack and pulled out a notebook and pen. "**On it!**" he said.

"We know that Tulip went missing sometime

after lunch today," I said.

"Most likely in the science lab," added Zoe.

We paused, because that was really all we knew.

"We also know that Mr. Dougal probably won't be able to find her," I said. "I mean, did you see his classroom?"

Zoe and Bernard nodded solemnly.

"And we know that we are probably the school's **ONLY HOPE** of finding the extremely dangerous, potentially **DEADLY** giant spider."

Bernard scrunched his face up in disagreement. "I don't think Tulip is a deadly spider," he said. "From everything I've read about spiders, and it's a lot, tarantulas **aren't** deadly to humans. I mean, if we were mice or birds, we would be in trouble."

I sighed. "Okay, fine. We are the school's **ONLY HOPE** of finding the **EXTREMELY DANGEROUS** and **VERY AGGRESSIVE** giant spider."

"Better," said Bernard, scribbling furiously on the pad of paper.

"Now what?" asked Zoe, crunching on a cracker.

"Hmmm," I said, looking up at the sky, hoping that inspiration would strike. **Captain Jane** on **SPACE BLASTERS** says you have to be prepared for inspiration to strike at **ANY** moment. I was hoping it would choose this moment, when I really needed it, to strike.

Just then something struck me right in my side and **knocked** me over onto the picnic blanket, sending jelly beans

68

scattering everywhere. "Oomph!" I said, as two sticky hands grabbed my face.

"WHAT'S THE EMERGENCY?"

Lucy shouted.

"Get off me," I grumbled, sitting up and pushing my little sister off. "And go back inside—we're having a very important meeting."

"I heard you in the parking lot," said Lucy, bouncing excitedly. "Talking about a secret **EMERGENCY** meeting you were going to have. I wanted to come straight out, but I had to have my snack first." She looked around at our now-scattered food. "If I'd known you had snacks out here, I would have come right away!"

"It's **top secret**, Lucy," I said. "We can't tell you. Sorry."

Lucy stamped her foot. "But I'm the **BEST** at top-secret emergencies. You know that."

I opened my mouth to argue, but then Zoe spoke up. "She's got a point, Sam," she said. "Lucy has come in pretty handy before."

Lucy beamed. "**Yeah!**" she said. "And Zoe even made me my own official ghost-hunter certificate, remember?"

It was true, she had.

"This is different, Lucy," I said. "It's the most **dangerous** mission we've ever attempted. You're my little sister—I have to protect you. It's my job."

"Can you at least tell me what it is?" said Lucy. "Please?"

"I have to consult my crew," I said, looking over at Zoe and Bernard.

"It can't hurt . . ." said Zoe.

Bernard nodded in agreement.

"Okay, Lucy," I said, lowering my voice. "But you have to pinky swear not to tell **ANYONE**, okay? It's top secret. We don't want anyone messing up our mission."

Lucy held out her little finger, and I grabbed it with my own, sealing our pinky promise.

"I don't want to scare you," I said, "but . . .

71

there's a **GIANT** spider on the loose at school."

Lucy looked at me expectantly. "And . . . it's radioactive?" she said.

I shook my head. "No . . ."

"And it's a **FLYING** spider?" she went on.

"No," I said.

"**A PEOPLE-EATING SPIDER?**" she said.

"Not exactly," I admitted.

"So you're saying just a regular spider is on the loose?" she said.

"I wouldn't call it a normal spider," Bernard clarified. "It's a Goliath birdeating tarantula, the biggest spider in the world."

"But it's still just a spider, right?"

"Right," I said, unsure why she wasn't more scared. I knew Lucy was brave, but surely this had to scare her at least a little bit. "But a **HUGE** one." I held out my hands to show her the size. "Bigger than your head!"

Lucy's eyes got huge, finally giving me the response I was expecting.

"Awesome," she breathed.

Zoe, Bernard, and I all looked at each other.

"Lucy," said Zoe. "Do you . . . like spiders?"

Lucy shook her head back and forth rapidly, her pigtails whipping in the air. "I don't **like** spiders," she said, "I **LOVE** spiders. I'm the Spider Queen!" She did a twirl.

"What?" we all said. Then I sighed.

"Lucy, this isn't a game. This is serious. There really is a giant spider on the loose at school."

"I know that," she said. "And I'm being serious too!" Then she leaned toward us and whispered, "Do you want me to show you my spider subjects?"

"Your **WHAT?**"

"I told you," she said, like it was the most obvious thing in the world, "I'm the Spider Queen. So of course I need spider subjects. Come on, follow me! But don't let anyone see where we go!" She skipped away to the bushes in the back of our garden. "**Come on**," she said in a loud whisper. Then

she got down on her hands and knees
and crawled into the bushes.

A second later, her head popped back out.
"Are you all coming or what?"

"Does she think this is a
game?" said Bernard.

"Only one way to find
out," I said.

We went to the edge of
the garden, and crawled into
the bushes after Lucy.

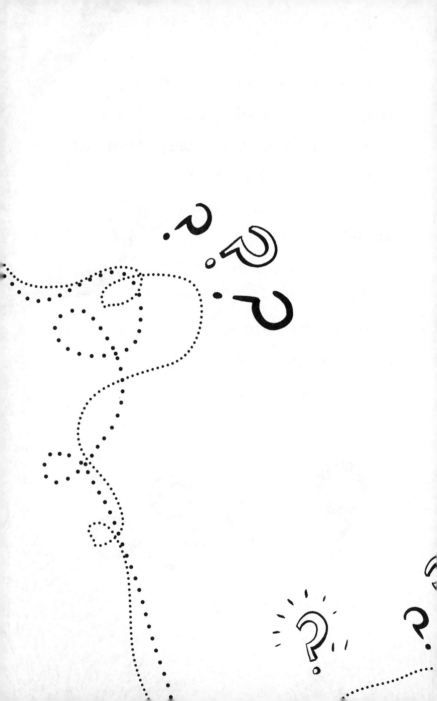

CHAPTER 7

SPIDER QUEEN

The tunnel through the bushes was small, and branches and thorns scratched my arms as we chased after Lucy.

Lucy is smaller than us, and the tunnel seemed **perfectly** shaped for her. "Almost there," she called out over her shoulder.

"Are we still even in your back garden?" Bernard asked from behind me.

He was breathing
heavily. "And *do*
you know how far
it goes?"

"I don't know," I said.
And then I suddenly remembered
Bernard didn't really like small spaces. "**Don't
worry**," I said as authoritatively as I could.
"We've got to be there soon!"

Then just as I had replied, the tunnel ended,
opening into a small dome-shaped clearing
edged entirely with bushes, all around and
above us. There was enough space for Lucy to
stand, but the rest of us had to crouch or sit.

"Welcome to my **spider court**," said Lucy,
picking up a crown made of leaves and
twigs and putting it on her head.

78

We just stared. Strung along all the branches and just above our heads were dozens of **glistening** spider webs.

Zoe crept backward till she was in the small tunnel we had come from. "I was not expecting this," she said.

"How did you find this?" I whispered. As my eyes adjusted to the dim light in the clearing, I could see **HUNDREDS** of spiders crawling all over the bushes.

Lucy shrugged. "I was just exploring in the garden one day, and then Butterbutt disappeared into the bushes, so I followed him. And then I found this spot! And it was **COVERED** in spiders! So I decided to become their queen," she said.

She held out a finger to one of the webs and a small black spider **crawled** on to her hand.

"This one is Itsy," she said. "You know, like the song '**Itsy Bitsy Spider**'?" Then she grinned at us. "I call most of them Itsy," she admitted. "Sometimes it's hard to tell them apart."

"But . . . but don't they ever bite you?"
I asked, swatting over my shoulder. I was sure
spiders were going to pounce on me from
every direction at any second. I wished
that *I* had eight eyes like the spiders so I
could be absolutely certain they weren't
about to jump on me. And it wasn't just me!
Zoe was still hovering around the tunnel
entrance like she was ready to make a quick
escape (this was actually very wise), and
Bernard still hadn't said a word—he just
stared all around him with **HUGE** eyes.

Lucy shrugged again. "You get mosquito
bites, don't you? It's the same thing."

"But, **LUCY**," I said. "Some spiders are
POISONOUS."

"None of my spiders are," she said confidently, putting Itsy back on a branch.

"You can't even tell them apart!" I sputtered. "How do you know none of them are **poisonous**?"

"I know black widow spiders have a red marking on them, and none of my spiders have that," said Lucy. "And all the really poisonous spiders live in Australia." She sighed. "Besides, if I thought a spider was going to bite me, I'd just **squash it**."

Zoe looked like she might throw up.

Then Butterbutt came bounding in. With a leap, he tore down one of the webs and caught one spider with his paw and one in his mouth.

"**Butterbutt!**" said Lucy, going over and
scooping him up, not even caring about the
spider webs getting all over her. "That isn't
very nice!" she scolded. But she didn't seem

too bothered that she'd just lost two of her spider subjects. "Butterbutt is **great** at catching spiders," said Lucy. "I'm trying to teach him how to catch and release, instead of catch and eat."

That was when the idea hit me. It was like **Captain Jane** says, **"Inspiration can strike at any time."** Although, I guess it did *kind* of make sense for me to get an idea on how to catch a spider while sitting in a spider den.

"Lucy," I said. "Do you think Butterbutt would be able to find the missing tarantula at school?"

"Butterbutt's a cat, **not** a bloodhound," said Zoe.

"But we know he's good at finding things," I said.

"How do we know that Butterbutt wouldn't, you know, **accidentally** try to eat Tulip?" said Bernard. "You heard what Lucy just said—she's trying to teach him to catch and release, not catch and eat."

"Tulip is too big for Butterbutt to swallow in one bite," I said. "If we stayed close, we could pull Butterbutt away before he did any harm."

"What about the damage Tulip could do to Butterbutt?" said Zoe.

"**Who's Tulip?**" asked Lucy, looking confused. She clutched Butterbutt to her chest. "I don't want Butterbutt to do anything **dangerous!**"

"Tulip is the missing giant tarantula," I said. "And as long as Tulip doesn't bite Butterbutt, he'll be okay."

"That won't be the only thing we have to worry about," said Bernard, making his extra-serious face. "I've read that tarantulas can release a shower of tiny **spiky hairs** into the air—we don't want Butterbutt to get in the way of those!"

I looked at Butterbutt. Butterbutt looked back at me. I felt like maybe he could understand how important this was. "Butterbutt is surprisingly smart, for a cat," I said. "He'd know to run away if Tulip started to attack like that."

"I know!" said Lucy. "I bet there are videos online of tarantulas **attacking!** We can show them to Butterbutt so he knows what to do."

"Lucy, Butterbutt *isn't* that smart," I said, frowning. "He's still just a cat."

"You are the one suggesting that Butterbutt can somehow find the spider," muttered Zoe.

"Butterbutt is a **VERY** smart cat," said Lucy, reaching out and grabbing Butterbutt from me. She held him protectively.

"Lucy might have a point," said Bernard. "Not that Butterbutt should watch the videos, but *we* should. So we know what to do."

I turned to Zoe. "Zoe, you're the fastest person in our grade. Do you think you could keep up with Butterbutt?"

Zoe nodded. "But I don't want to get anywhere near Tulip," she said. She shuddered. **"I think I'm allergic to spiders**. Especially ones that can send their spiky hairs into the air."

"That's okay," I said. "We'll be right behind you—we just need to make sure we don't lose Butterbutt." I looked at the cat. "And I've got the **perfect** idea to make sure that Butterbutt doesn't get bitten."

"Great," said Zoe. "Now that we've got a plan, can we get out of here? I feel like I've got spiders crawling all over me!"

"You probably do," said Lucy. "But **don't worry**, they're easy to brush off, and they *almost* never bite."

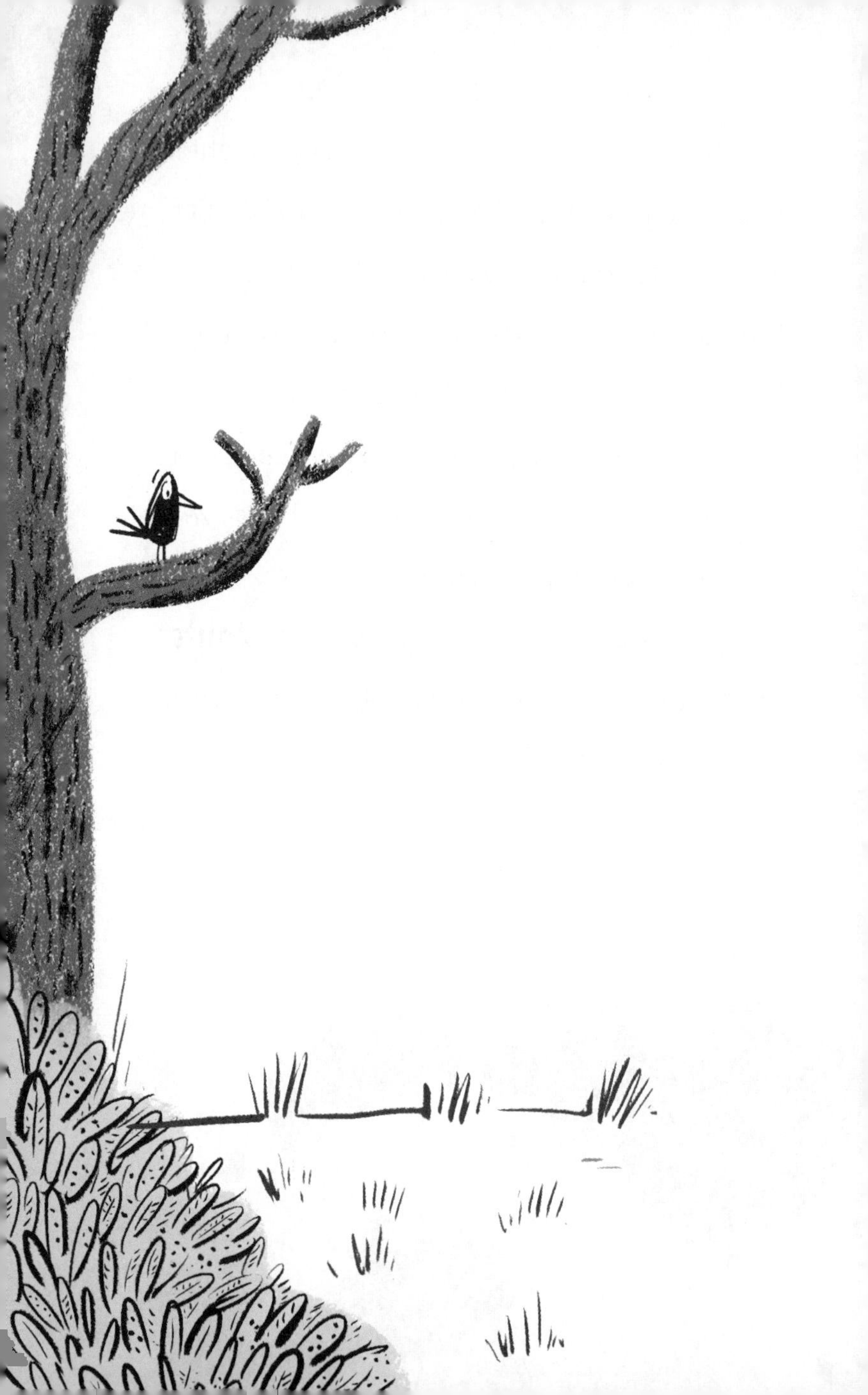

CHAPTER 8

THE MASTER PLAN

We crawled back into the main area of our garden just in time. Na-Na, my grandma, was coming out to do some gardening. She looked at us suspiciously.

"**Where have you been?**" she asked.

"Just playing, Na-Na," I said.

"Hmmm," she said.

"I showed Sam my spiders!" said Lucy.

"Lucy," I whispered, "the spider thing is a secret, remember?"

"Oh, I know all about Lucy the **Spider**

Queen," said Na-Na. "You can't hide anything from me, remember?"

I nodded. It is true. Na-Na can hear **EVERYTHING,** and she has a spooky ability to know when we are up to something.

But the good thing is, she usually helps us out if we ask nicely. After all, she was the one I convinced to buy me my pet snake when I knew my parents would say no. All it took was promising to weed her garden. Na-Na is sometimes susceptible to bribes.

"What secret spider thing are you talking about, Sam?" Na-Na said, narrowing her eyes at me.

"Nothing," I said quickly.

"Hmm," she said. "Well, you know I'll find out anyway."

Then she went into her gardening shed, put on her giant gardening gloves, and grabbed her gardening scissors. "Lucy," she said over her shoulder, "tell your little **spider friends** I'm pruning the bushes today, so they'd better run away if they don't want to get **chopped**."

Then she started whacking away at the bushes.

"I'm glad we aren't still in those bushes," said Bernard, "otherwise we might have been the ones getting chopped!"

We all went up into my room and turned on my computer. It only took Bernard a few seconds to find hundreds of videos of tarantulas doing all kinds of **crazy things**—catching prey, making webs, and, just what we were looking for, going into battle with a bigger animal.

In one video, a small leopard came close, but before it could attack, the tarantula started shooting its spiky hairs everywhere—and the leopard **ran away**!

Lucy tried to get Butterbutt to watch the videos, but as usual, he was **much** more interested in watching Fang in his enclosure. He kept batting at the side of the glass.

"Lucy," I said, "keep an eye on Butterbutt."

"Maybe we should bring Fang to school to catch Tulip," suggested Zoe.

The idea of both a spider and a snake on the loose at school did **NOT** seem like a good plan.

"Remember the time Fang went missing in the house and we couldn't find him?" I said. "There is no way we'd be able to find him if he got lost at school. At least we know we won't lose Butterbutt."

"You'd better **not** lose Butterbutt," said Lucy.

"We won't," I said. "That's all part of my master plan."

"What is this master plan?" said Zoe. "You still haven't told us."

"We need a few things first," I said. "A small bell, some string, and lots of tinfoil."

"Tinfoil?" said Bernard. And then his face

lit up. "Of course! To make a protective suit!"

"Exactly!" I said with a grin. "And the bell will be so we don't lose Butterbutt. The string is to tie the bell on him."

I lowered my voice to a whisper. "We'll have to do all this at school though, and the hardest part is going to be sneaking Butterbutt in." I looked at Lucy. "Lucy, I was hoping you could help with that." Lucy had experience sneaking Butterbutt into places that he wasn't supposed to go. My bedroom, the beach, the grocery store, the library, **her karate class**—and lots of places I probably didn't even know about.

She nodded, beaming. "I told you I could help out with the mission!" she said.

"Great," I said. "Then it's a plan. Tomorrow

morning, we'll all meet at our spot by the fence."

"I don't know where that is," said Lucy.

"That's okay," I said, "we can meet outside the kindergarten class instead. And then we'll wrap Butterbutt in tinfoil, tie the bell on him, and let him find Tulip! It's a **foolproof plan.**"

Bernard frowned. "I don't know, Sam," he said. "Won't there be teachers and students everywhere?"

"Good point," I said. "Maybe we all get to school early and sneak in before class starts."

"*Now* it's a foolproof plan," said Bernard.

"There are about a **MILLION** things that could go wrong!" exclaimed Zoe. "We're leaving everything down to Butterbutt?"

"Do you have any other ideas?" I asked.

Zoe frowned. "No, but I don't love this one."

"Well, as **Spaceman Jack** says, **'Sometimes it's better to go with the bad idea you've got, than the good idea you haven't thought of.'"**

"That's a terrible saying," said Zoe.

"And that's what **Captain Jane** says whenever he says it," I said. "But in this case, I think we've got to agree with him." I put my hand out in front of me. "This will only work if **we're all in it together**. Are you with me?"

Bernard stuck his hand in.

Then Lucy grabbed Butterbutt and made him stick his paw in, which he did with a yowl.

YOWWWL!

I looked at Zoe. "We need you, Zoe. You're the only one fast enough to keep up with Butterbutt."

Zoe sighed dramatically. "I don't know what you would all do without me," she said. But then she grinned and put her hand in. "I'm in."

"**For the universe!**" we all shouted and shot our hands up into the air like rockets.

I just knew our plan would work.

CHAPTER 9

FRIED RICE AND FISH EYES

Before we went down for dinner, we made sure to wash our hands extra carefully. After all, we'd been crawling around in a spider den. And I didn't want to accidentally eat any **spider germs**.

"Are we having roast duck for dinner again?" asked Zoe as we went downstairs. "I really liked that the last time I was here for dinner!"

I smiled at her, remembering how my friends had been **really** nervous about trying my favorite dinner, roast duck and turnip cake, but had then ended up liking it.

"Tonight we're having **MY** favorite dinner," said Lucy. "Whole fish!"

"I can't eat a whole fish myself," Bernard said, sounding anxious.

I laughed. "Don't worry," I said. "It's for all of us. My dad will help get the bones out. too."

"There are **BONES** in fish?" said Zoe. "I've only had fish fingers."

"Of course there are bones in fish," I said.

Zoe shrugged. "I mean, Bernard did say today that spiders don't use muscles. It wouldn't be that crazy if fish didn't have bones."

"I'm sure some fish don't have bones," said Bernard thoughtfully. "I wonder if **octopuses** have bones."

"We aren't having octopus," I said. "We're having fish with garlic and ginger."

We sat down at the table just as my dad was finishing the fried rice.

103

"I love an audience when I cook!" he said. "Everyone watching?"

I groaned—my dad loves to pretend he's a contestant on a TV cooking competition. But Bernard and Zoe watched with wide eyes as he turned the fire under the wok up high and **flipped** the fried rice. He doesn't usually put on so much of a show, but I knew he wanted to impress my friends.

Zoe and Bernard applauded when he was done.

My dad put fried rice in everyone's bowls. In addition to the rice and the fish, we also had **Chinese broccoli** in a **garlic sauce**.

"I'll portion out the fish for everyone," said my dad.

"Sam," whispered Bernard, kicking me under

the table, "the fish is **STARING** at me."

"If you don't like it looking at you," said
Na-Na, "I can help with that." Then she reached
across with her chopsticks, plucked out the
eyeball, and popped it in her mouth.

I groaned. Zoe and Bernard stared open-mouthed.

"You **don't** know what you're missing," Na-Na said with a grin. "But my favorite part is the cheek," she added, and then took that, too.

"Don't worry," I reassured Zoe and Bernard, "the rest of the fish just tastes like . . . well, **delicious** garlic and ginger fish."

"I can't believe your grandma just ate a fish eyeball," said Bernard.

"I can," said Zoe, looking at Na-Na with new-found respect.

Luckily, **everyone** liked the fish. And everything else! After dinner, we had ice cream and watched an episode of SPACE BLASTERS. It was a very good evening.

And tomorrow we'd go into school and **save the day**.

CHAPTER 10

BUTTERBUTT THE BURRITO CAT

My mom couldn't believe it when Lucy and I were up and ready to go to school by the time she came downstairs the next morning.

"We've already had our breakfast," I said proudly. **"I made cereal."**

"Well done, Sam," said my mom. "I've never

seen you two get ready for school so fast."

"I have a test, and I don't want to be late,"
I said. It wasn't **totally** true[7] and I felt bad
for telling my mom a lie, but I didn't know what
else to do.

"And I want to see my friends before class,"
said Lucy.

"I'm **not** complaining," said my mom. "I'm
just glad I didn't have to drag you both out of
bed like I usually *do* in the morning!"

I thought we were in the clear till we got in
the car. Butterbutt chose that moment to
start meowing from inside Lucy's backpack.

MeeeooOOwwwwwWW!

---

[7] It wasn't true at all.

Luckily, I was sitting in the front seat, so I turned on the radio **super** loud.

"Sam!" Mom said, wincing at the music and turning it down. "That's way too loud."

"I like it!" shouted Lucy.

"You don't even know this song," said my mom, laughing.

"I don't know it, but I like it!" Lucy yelled.

Between Lucy's shouting, the music, and the rumbling of the car, you could barely hear Butterbutt.

As soon as we pulled up to the school, we hopped out of the car before my mom had a chance to hear the tiniest meow.

Lucy unzipped her backpack and let Butterbutt poke his head out.

"I had to take **all my books** out of my backpack," she said. "I'll have to tell my teacher I forgot them."

I felt a little bit bad for dragging Lucy into all this. The last thing I wanted was for her to get in trouble.

"Thanks for helping us, Lucy," I said. "You're a real member of the team now."

She **beamed**.

"Now let's go find Zoe and Bernard," I said with a smile.

It turned out that Butterbutt did *not* like getting wrapped in tinfoil.

"Hold still," I said, trying to wrap tinfoil

around his front leg. "This is for your own **protection!**"

"You'd better hurry up," said Bernard, looking at his watch. "School starts in ten minutes. We don't have much time to sneak in before everyone goes inside."

In the end, I had to wrap Butterbutt up like a burrito and leave his head, legs, and tail sticking out.

A small bell hung around his neck. He glared at me and whisked his tail back and forth to show **exactly** how much he did not like his protective suit. "I'm sorry, Butterbutt," I said. "It's for your own protection. And if you behave, I'll give you lots of treats after school today."

Butterbutt swatted at me.

Lucy grabbed Butterbutt up and looked directly in his eyes. "Okay, Butterbutt," she said. "It's **very** important for you to find the tarantula. Do you understand?"

"Of course he doesn't understand," said Zoe. "He's a cat."

"He understands." Lucy scowled. "I **know** he does."

"Okay, crew," I said before a fight broke out over how smart Butterbutt actually was.

"We don't have much time. **Are we ready?**"

Everyone nodded.

We crept to the door and slowly pulled it open.

"The coast is clear," said Bernard, peeking in.

Lucy put Butterbutt on the floor inside the school. Butterbutt didn't go anywhere, but meowed and turned around, headbutting Lucy's shin.

MeeeooOOwwwwwwW!

"Go on, Butterbutt!" I said. I didn't know what would happen if other kids started to come in.

He just stared up at me.

"I thought you said this was a **foolproof plan**," said Zoe.

I was starting to sweat. "Come on, Butterbutt," I said, leaning down and nudging him forward.

Then his ears perked up, and he got his **ninja-cat** expression. His whiskers twitched.

"I think he senses Tulip!" I said excitedly.

And then Butterbutt shot off down the hall, just as the first bell rang and kids swarmed in.

"After that cat!" I yelled, chasing him down the hall. Zoe raced ahead of me. More and more kids were coming in from all directions, and it was almost **impossible** to dodge them.

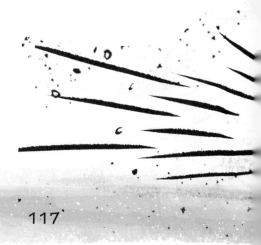

117

Butterbutt ran between their legs. I could hear people exclaiming as a cat wrapped in **tinfoil** ran by them.

"Where's he going?" I huffed.

Lucy and Bernard were right behind me. And Butterbutt was still in our line of sight— just. The second bell rang. If the third bell rang and we weren't in class, we would all be in a lot of trouble. But we **couldn't** stop now!

Just then Butterbutt turned a corner and scrambled into an open door. There was a shout. We all ran after the sound and into the room.

"That's my classroom!" said Lucy.
We **ran** in and the whole class
stared at us.

Lucy's teacher was so
surprised by our entrance, even she
just stared at us!

"We'll just be a minute," I said, frantically
looking around. "Sorry to interrupt, class.
Back to . . . erm . . . whatever you were doing."

"Lucy Wu, **what's going on?**" spluttered
her teacher.

"She's helping us with a very important mission, miss!" I said.

"Well, it's funny you ask that, miss," said Lucy, "because it's a really long story and **FIRST OF ALL** . . ."

While Lucy kept her teacher occupied with the longest explanation in the world about exactly what we were all up to (none of which was true), I looked madly round the classroom for Butterbutt—without any luck. Where was he?

But then there was a commotion in the corner. I swung round to see Butterbutt crouched right next to the class rabbit cage, **swatting** at the door.

"Butterbutt can't open that, can he?" said Bernard nervously.

I shook my head and dashed forward. We

didn't have time for Butterbutt to be distracted by a bunny rabbit.

Somehow by the time I got to Butterbutt, he *had* managed to open the rabbit's cage! The bunny came **bounding** out, and Butterbutt started to chase it around the room and under tables and chairs.

"Oh no," I moaned.

All the kids in the class began screaming and either jumping up on tables or running after Butterbutt and the rabbit in a crazy kind of chase. The teacher, who had just figured out what had happened, shouted, **"Someone close the door!"**

But it was too late—Butterbutt had chased the bunny out into the hall.

Just as the third bell rang.

"I'll get them!" cried Zoe, and she leaped over two kids and into the hall.

We all ran after her. And I mean *everyone.* The **entire class** ran out into the hall after Butterbutt and the bunny, with Zoe leading the way. There was a trail of tinfoil scattered all along the hallway floor, so I knew we were going the right direction.

The teacher was still shouting, but nobody

was listening to her. Other classroom doors opened to see what all the commotion was, and then Butterbutt **chased** the bunny into another class!

There were shouts of surprise, and then Zoe ran in, with me right behind her. I turned into the classroom just in time to see Zoe dive on top of the rabbit. "Sam!" Zoe yelled. "Grab Butterbutt!"

I flung myself forward and snatched up Butterbutt in my arms. He yowled loudly and wiggled, but I had a good grip on him.

Lucy's teacher burst into the room, holding Lucy by the hand.

"What is going on here?" she demanded.

Lucy and I stared at each other, and I wished that we could communicate telepathically like sometimes they can do on SPACE BLASTERS.

I couldn't let Lucy take all the blame herself. Especially because this whole thing was my fault.

"It was my idea," I said, jumping in. "I thought we could dress up our cat like an **astronaut** and then Lucy could bring him in for show-and-tell."

Lucy's teacher frowned. "Sam Wu, I don't think it's very sensible to dress your cat up in tinfoil, let alone bring it to school."

I shrugged. "It seemed like a good idea at the time." Which was sort of true. Even though we knew bringing Butterbutt to school hadn't been the best idea, it was the only idea we'd been able to come up with. We had no idea it was going to go **so wrong**.

"Miss," said Zoe, holding the **squirming** rabbit, "where should I put this bunny?"

"We'll need to bring it back to our classroom," said the teacher. "And the cat, too, I suppose."

"I can take Butterbutt!" said Lucy, reaching out to me.

Butterbutt calmed down once Lucy was holding him.

"Lucy," said her teacher, "I'm going to have to call your parents and ask them to come get your cat. Can you please wait up in the office?"

"Am I **in trouble**?" Lucy asked, her lower lip trembling.

Her teacher sighed. "No," she said. "But next time, please ask permission first. From both me and your parents."

Lucy nodded.

I felt **awful**.

"It's because I brought my snake to school once," I said. "So I thought it would be okay."

"Sounds like you have quite the **zoo** at your house," said Lucy's teacher with a smile. "Now, you three . . ."

She glanced around, but there was no sign of Bernard. "I **swear** there were three of you."

"Right here, miss!" said Bernard, running up behind us. "Sorry, I was in the bathroom."

I frowned. Bernard had also gone to the bathroom while I'd been wrapping Butterbutt in tinfoil. He must have drunk **a lot** of juice at breakfast.

"You three should get to your class. Thank you for helping us catch the cat and the rabbit. I'll write your teacher a note to explain why you are late. And I'll take the rabbit," Lucy's teacher said, reaching for it from Zoe.

"Thanks, Lucy," I whispered as we walked past her. She grinned and raised her finger in the air like a **rocket ship** taking off. It took me a second, and then I realized she was doing the **for the universe** gesture from

SPACE BLASTERS! I didn't even know that she knew it. She must have been paying more attention than I'd thought.

I grinned and did it back.

CHAPTER 11

A NEW PLAN

Ms. Winkleworth was very confused about why my sister had brought her cat to school, but at least we didn't get in trouble for being late.

But we still were **nowhere** close to catching Tulip! I knew we had to come up with a new plan.

At recess we met at our usual spot by the fence.

"Well," said Zoe. "That didn't go as planned."

We all looked at each other and burst out

laughing. In hindsight[8] it really had been a **terrible** idea to bring Butterbutt to school to help us catch Tulip.

"I can't believe we didn't get in trouble!" I said once we'd stopped laughing.

Just then, Regina ran toward us. "What happened?" she asked breathlessly. "Did you find Tulip? I'm sorry I couldn't come over yesterday to help come up with a plan!"

"That's okay," I said with a smile. "And no, we haven't found Tulip."

"Do you think she is still on the loose?" said Regina with **wide eyes**.

Bernard nodded. "I can, in fact, confirm that she is. I didn't actually go to the bathroom earlier while you were chasing Butterbutt and

---

[8] I learned this from **SPACE BLASTERS**—it means when you look back on something that has already happened.

the bunny. I went to the sixth grade science lab. I thought I should just check to see if Tulip had been found." He lowered his voice. "Her tank is **still** empty, and Mr. Dougal looked like he had been up all night searching for her!"

"Excellent investigating!" I said, giving Bernard a high five.

Bernard grinned at me. "I thought it was the most logical thing to do. No point in looking for a spider that has already been found."

"So what now?" asked Regina.

"**The search must go on**," I declared. "We just need another plan." I wasn't going to give up now. Not after I had decided that we had to be the ones to find Tulip. If I caught a missing giant spider, nobody could ever call me Scaredy-Cat Sam again!

"A better plan," said Zoe.

"Do you remember, when we were trying
to catch the ghost in Sam's
house, how we used honey?"
said Bernard slowly.

Zoe **groaned**. "Honey
isn't going to attract
a spider."

"It might!" said Bernard.
"And remember, we said that
everything likes honey. Why not spiders?
What's that saying? You catch more flies with
honey than vinegar?"

"I've never heard that saying," I said.

"My dad says it," said Bernard. "I'm not sure
what it means, but I know it is true. Anyway,

what do all spiders like? **Even tarantulas?**
FLIES. We don't need the honey to attract
the actual spider—we use it to catch flies,
and then those flies will attract Tulip! And as
an added bonus, the honey will work like a Tulip
trap, too. Even if Tulip doesn't get stuck in it,
she will leave a honey trail and we can follow it
to wherever she's hiding!"

"Bernard," I said. "You're a **genius!**"

"I know," said Bernard with a smile.

"So we're just going to dump honey all
over the school and hope for the best?" said
Zoe, throwing her hands up in the air. "This
might be an even worse plan than sending
Butterbutt in to school after Tulip!"

"That's **not** the whole plan," said Bernard,
sounding a little defensive. "We'll also have to

get Tulip back into her cage once we catch her."

"We'll obviously need protective gear," I said.

"Can you get some kind of gloves tonight?"

Bernard nodded. "My dad will definitely have gloves I can use." Bernard's dad is a palaeontologist, and he spends a lot of time looking at dusty **dinosaur bones** and **fossils**.

"I'll try to find some at my house," said Regina.

"My brothers probably have some kind of sports gloves I can steal," said Zoe. "So this is our plan? Use honey to catch Tulip, and then use gloves to pick her up?"

The thought of actually picking up Tulip the tarantula made me feel a bit queasy, but I swallowed hard. "I think that's the best plan we've got."

"Are we sure it **has** to be us who catch Tulip?" said Zoe.

I took a deep breath. I knew we couldn't give up. I knew *I* couldn't give up. **Spaceman Jack** never gives up. I gestured around at the rest of the school yard. "Who else is going to do it? Mr. Dougal clearly can't. And I **don't** see anyone else trying. It has to be us. We're the only ones with the proper experience."

"We don't have any spider-catching experience!" said Zoe.

"But we've got all kinds of other experience that has prepared us for this," I said. "We've outsmarted sharks—"

"You have?" said Regina with wide eyes.

"**Not exactly**," said Zoe. "We just didn't get eaten by any."

"I think that counts as outsmarting them," said Bernard.

I cleared my throat and went on with my inspirational speech. "We've hunted **ghosts**, wrangled **snakes**, and solved mysteries in the dark! It's like when **Spaceman Jack** encounters a new species of alien. Even if he hasn't met that exact kind of alien yet, he has experience from other planets that he can use."

Zoe frowned. "I don't know if that totally makes sense, but I guess you're right."

I beamed. "**SPACE BLASTERS** is always right."

"There's only one small issue with this plan," said Bernard. "Where are we going to get all the honey that we need?"

"Leave that to me," I said. "I know **just** the place."

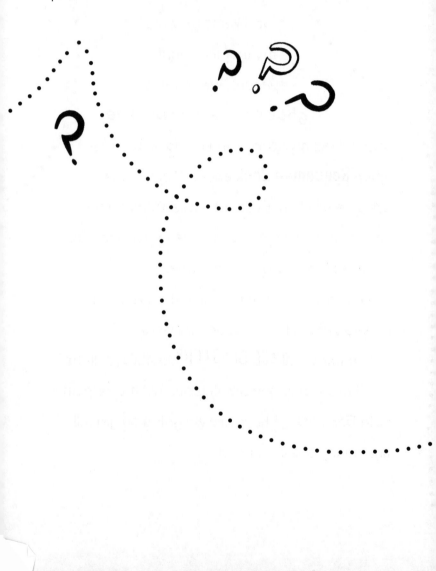

CHAPTER 12

THE BEEKEEPER

After school I went into the garden to find
Na-Na.

"Na-Na," I said, "can we go to visit your
friend Melinda?"

Na-Na paused her digging and looked up at
me. "**Why?**" she asked.

I've learned that sometimes it is best to be
honest with Na-Na.

"There's a giant spider on the loose at
school. I need to catch it, and Bernard thinks

we should use honey. I know Melinda has a **LOT** of honey." I eyed Na-Na's gardening gloves. "Also, could I borrow your gardening gloves?"

"You know, your sister is great with spiders," said Na-Na.

I nodded. "I know," I said. "But this spider is bigger than her whole head. I don't think it's a job for her."

"But it's a job for you?" asked Na-Na, sounding **dubious**.

I nodded again, more vigorously this time.

"Well," said Na-Na, putting down her gardening shovel, "I can take you to Melinda, and I can lend you my gloves, but you know it's going to cost you."

That's the thing with Na-Na—she never does **anything** for free.

"I know," I said.

She looked up at the sky and did some rapid Na-Na calculations in her head. "One week of weeding the garden, **AND** you have to go with me to the market this weekend and help me carry the groceries."

I stuck my hand out. It was a **good deal**.

Na-Na grinned. "Let me wash my hands and then call Melinda to see if she's home."

Melinda is Na-Na's best friend. She lives on the next street over. She's got an even bigger garden than Na-Na and is always making **concoctions** from the things she grows. Soups, candles, lotions—all kinds of things! She might be a wizard. But she also might be a spy—she seems to know everything that is happening in the neighborhood.

She is also a beekeeper. She had to get special permission to have a small hive in her garden. But Na-Na says nobody, not even the city council, says no to Melinda. So I knew she would have **plenty of honey**.

Melinda was home, so Na-Na and I walked over together. It was a sunny day, and if I hadn't been so stressed about the spider on the loose, I **might** have asked if we could go to the park, too.

We knocked on her door, and Melinda let us in. "I hear you want some of my honey?"

I started to explain to Melinda why I needed honey, but she interrupted me. "I know all about the spider," she said. "Tulip, is it?"

Like I said, Melinda knows **everything**.

"Hmmm," she went on, looking at Na-Na. "I have to say, this is a most unusual plan. But the best ones usually are. Just make sure you don't tell anyone that Na-Na and I helped you."

I crossed my heart.

"Very good," she said. "Now, do you want to go and say hello to my bees?"

I shook my head. "No, thank you," I said as politely as I could. I'd had **enough** trouble with creatures this week, what with all the spiders. I didn't want to add bees into the mix! But I also didn't want to offend Melinda or her bees. "Maybe next time?"

"Very well," said Melinda. "And you're in luck—I happen to have a few extra jars of honey. But you know if I give them to you . . ."

"I'll **owe you**," I finished. Melinda operates on the same system as Na-Na.

"He's very good at weeding the garden," Na-Na offered.

"I'm sure I can think of something," said Melinda.

She went into her kitchen and came back with three jars of **gleaming honey**. I put them in my backpack slowly, thinking about how to best approach my next request. "Thank you, Melinda," I said. "Um . . ."

"Yes, Sam? I can tell you want to ask me something else," said Melinda.

"What is it, Sam?" asked Na-Na. "Melinda has already been very generous."

"Can I borrow your **beekeeper helmet**?" I burst out, deciding it was best to get straight to the point.

Melinda raised her eyebrows. "What for?" she asked.

I explained about the tarantula's secret super power to send spikes of hair into the air. "It seems sensible to protect my face."

Melinda tapped her chin. "Very well," she said. "But I expect you to bring it back to me **tomorrow**, do you understand?"

"Thank you, Melinda!" I said.

Melinda smiled. "You're very welcome, Sam."

Something else occurred to me. I looked from Na-Na to Melinda. "You two won't tell my parents about any of this, will you?"

"Something tells me this plan of yours might just stress your parents out, and I have a feeling you'll find a way to do it no matter what. So, we'll keep this a **secret**," said Na-Na. Then her face grew serious. "But be careful, Sam. Back in Hong Kong, I came across lots of spiders. Tarantulas, jumping spiders, giant huntsman spiders, and huge banana spiders. Spiders are to be respected."

"Spiders that live in **bananas**?" I asked.

Na-Na shook her head. "Spiders as big as bananas."

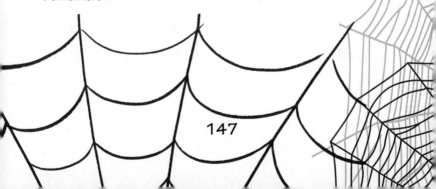

147

"Sometimes spiders do hide in bananas though," added Melinda.

I gulped. I was glad that Tulip wasn't a jumping spider. At least we had a chance of catching her if she stayed on the ground. And I would start examining bananas with **extra care** now, too.

Melinda brought me her beekeeper helmet. It was heavier than I expected and hard to see out of, but it was the **perfect** spider protection.

"When you return my helmet, you'll have to tell me how your adventure went. Good luck, Sam."

I almost did my **"for the universe"** hand rocket signal, but then I remembered Melinda probably wouldn't know what that was. So instead I just shook her hand and said thank you again.

I knew I was as ready as I'd ever be.

CHAPTER 13

THE TRAP

I met Zoe and Bernard at our spot by the fence the next day before school. I'd told my mom that I was bringing the beekeeper hat into school for a project about bees.

"Your school has **a lot** of interesting projects," she'd said, raising an eyebrow, but luckily she hadn't asked any more questions. She had, however, checked Lucy's backpack to make sure she wasn't trying to smuggle

Butterbutt into school again.

"Sam," said Bernard seriously, while inspecting my beekeeper hat, "you know that you are going to have to be the one to **actually** catch Tulip. Because you have the best protective gear."

It was true, I did. All Bernard had been able to find at home were basic plastic gloves that his dad used while cleaning fossils. Zoe had a pair of her older brother's ski gloves, but they were too big and made her hands bulky.

"We'll help you, of course," said Zoe, looking a bit relieved.

We decided not to go in before school started like we had yesterday. Today we were going to **sneak** in from the playground during recess, and hope that would give us enough

152

time to set our honey traps and find Tulip.

Recess was only twenty minutes long, so every minute would count.

"What happens if we can't find Tulip in time?" Zoe asked.

"We come back in at lunch and look again," I said. "The honey traps will have **definitely** caught Tulip by then."

"But won't someone clean up the honey while we're in class?" asked Zoe. I frowned—I hadn't thought of that.

"I know!" said Bernard. "We'll put up signs next to the honey, saying it's for a science experiment and to leave it there."

"**Brilliant!**" I said.

This was definitely going to work, I was sure of it.

It was very hard to concentrate that morning in class.

While we were working on spelling, Regina came over to my desk. "Sam," she whispered. "I couldn't find **any** gloves at home!" Then she lowered her voice even more. "And I think Ralph knows that we're up to something."

I looked over at Ralph, and sure enough, he was glaring at me over his assignment.

"Since I don't have gloves anyway, I thought maybe I could lead Ralph off the trail. Make sure he doesn't follow you guys," said Regina. "We don't want him to spoil the plan."

"Regina, that's **genius!**" I said. I tried to snap my fingers, but I don't know how, so it didn't have the effect I was hoping for. But at least now we wouldn't have to worry about Ralph.

"I'm glad I can still be a part of the mission," said Regina.

"A **VERY** important part," I said. "And don't worry—you do your part, and we'll handle the rest."

Regina grinned. "Good luck, Sam."

Finally, it was recess. Instead of running outside like we usually did, Zoe, Bernard, and I lingered in the classroom. I saw Ralph eyeing us **suspiciously**, but then Regina

went over to him.

"Ralph," she said loudly, "will you come

to the front office with me? I have to call Mom—I think she forgot to pack our lunch."

"**No** lunch?" exclaimed Ralph. "I thought she put it in my backpack this morning."

Regina shook her head solemnly. "Well, I don't have any and even if you do, you'll have to **split it** with me."

Ralph's face dropped. **He does not like sharing food**. "Okay, I'll go with you to the office." He didn't even look back at us as he hurried after Regina.

"Out the rest of you go," Ms. Winkleworth said as she became distracted by something on her computer. We seized our chance and **raced** down the hall, away from our classroom, and toward Mr. Dougal's science lab. We had figured it would be best to start near where Tulip had last been spotted. Bernard poked his head in and confirmed that there was no sign of Mr. Dougal— or Tulip.

Then we started setting our honey traps. We each had a jar of Melinda's honey and a stack of papers that said **HONEY IS**

FOR SCIENCE EXPERIMENT—DO NOT CLEAN UP. Bernard had made them during class after he finished his spelling assignment. He has the neatest handwriting of us all.

We went along the hallway, pouring out **puddles** of honey in corners that looked like they might be appealing to spiders.

"We'll have to retrace our steps," said Bernard, "to see if our traps have caught anything!"

HONEY IS FOR
SCIENCE
EXPERIMENT –
DO NOT CLEAN UP

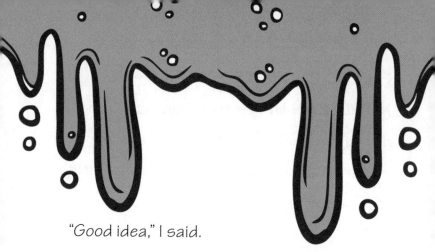

"Good idea," I said.

We reached the end of the hallway and were about to turn back around to check our traps, when I noticed a supply closet door propped open by a mop.

"Maybe we should put a trap in here," I said, **poking** my head inside. "It looks like the kind of place a spider might like." Bernard and Zoe followed me in. But as Bernard stepped inside, he fell into the mop, knocking it over and out of the way of the door.

Which then **slammed** shut.

"Whoops," he said.

Zoe went to open the door.

It didn't budge.

She pushed harder.

SLAM

The door stayed shut. She turned to us with wide eyes. "I think we're locked in!"

"There's no way we're locked in," I said. "Your hands just must be slippery from all the honey. Here, let me try."

I took off one of Na-Na's gardening gloves and **yanked** on the doorknob. It didn't move. I gulped. Zoe was right. We were completely locked in.

Bernard started to turn very pale. If he

161

hadn't liked being in the bushes in my back garden, he really wasn't going to like this. He doesn't even like playing **hide-and-seek**.

"It's okay, Bernard," I said loudly. I was speaking that way to try to show how calm and confident I was, even though my heart was beating so fast and loud in my chest, I was sure my friends could hear it. "Just take deep breaths."

I took my own advice and paused to take a **few long breaths**. I could feel myself starting to panic, but I could tell Bernard was more than scared. He was terrified, and I knew I had to be brave for him.

"Hey, you guys," said Zoe in a high voice.

"We're taking deep breaths," I said.

"Okay, but can you take deep breaths and also **LOOK OVER HERE!**" Zoe sounded even more panicked than Bernard.

I looked across and saw that Zoe had hopped up on top of a small footstool. And there, **right in the middle** of the supply closet, staring at all of us with her eight eyes, was Tulip.

CHAPTER 14

LOCKED IN

"WE FOUND TULIP!" Zoe shouted, as if it wasn't obvious.

I didn't know what to do. We'd achieved our goal of finding Tulip, but now we were **LOCKED IN A CLOSET WITH A GIANT TARANTULA**. I was feeling extremely unprepared. And to make matters worse, I could hear Bernard starting to panic-breathe next to me.

"SLOW, deep breaths, Bernard," I said.

He looked like he was almost about to cry.

"But, Sam," he said. "We're **LOCKED IN**."

"**WITH A GIANT SPIDER**,"

Zoe added. She started coughing. "I think I'm allergic to Tulip. I can't get any closer."

I didn't want to get any nearer to Tulip either, but I knew it had to be me. I was the one who needed to prove I wasn't a scaredy-cat after all.

I imagined what **Spaceman Jack** would do. He'd do what had to be done. I put on my beekeeper helmet and the gardening glove I'd taken off.

Tulip raised her front legs and

started hissing.

I began to sweat.

"Quick, Sam! Before she disappears somewhere in here," Zoe said. She was standing on her toes on the footstool, as far away from Tulip as she could get. I was almost surprised she hadn't started climbing up the shelves lining the small supply closet.

"But I **don't know** what to do!" I wailed.

"Well, what was your grand plan?" said Zoe.

Bernard had stopped speaking and was just standing with his back to a shelf, mumbling to himself.

"It definitely didn't involve being locked in a closet," I said.

"Here!" said Zoe, reaching up and grabbing a bucket from a shelf. "**Use this!**" She tossed the bucket to me, and I caught it.

I held the bucket out toward Tulip, who was still hissing. She started to back away from me, and I knew I had to be fast.

I lunged forward and threw the bucket on top of her. **Success!** We'd trapped Tulip!

Zoe cheered, and even Bernard managed a shaky thumbs-up.

But then the bucket **BEGAN TO MOVE**. "Ahh!" yelled Zoe.

"**AHH!**" I yelled.

Bernard might have been yelling, too, but no sound actually came out of his mouth, and his eyes looked like they were about to **pop out** of his head.

"Quick," said Zoe. "You have to sit on the bucket to keep Tulip from **GETTING AWAY!**"

The last thing I wanted to do was get any closer to the bucket—or Tulip—but I knew Zoe was right. I skirted around the bucket a bit, wiggling my bottom into the right position, and then sat down on top of it. I **shivered** as I heard Tulip scuttling around inside it, but at least the bucket wasn't moving any more.

"Now what?" said Zoe.

"We're going to be trapped in here forever!" Bernard wailed.

"No we aren't," I said. "Someone will come in eventually. You two, bang on the door and shout as loudly as you can!" I looked at Bernard. "You have to do it, Bernard. It's the only way we'll get out!"

Zoe hopped off the footstool. "Come on, Bernard," she said. And then she started banging on the door with her fists and yelling as **loudly** as she could.

Bernard began shouting, too.

And even though I couldn't help bang on the door because I had to stay sitting on the bucket so Tulip didn't escape again, I yelled, too.

Zoe found another bucket and used that to hit the door, which was **way louder** than her fists had been.

173

It was so loud inside the closet, I could barely hear myself think! I just hoped that someone outside could hear us, too.

And then just as I started to think that we were going to end up having a closet sleepover with a **GIANT SPIDER**, the door began to open.

Zoe and Bernard jumped back out of the way. A familiar face appeared.

"What is *going on* in here?"

CHAPTER 15

OFFICIAL SPIDER-CATCHER CLUB

I never thought I would be so happy to see Mr. Dougal!

I almost jumped off the bucket right then and there, but remembered I needed to stay put so Tulip wouldn't get out.

Bernard didn't wait another second—he pushed past Mr. Dougal and ran out into the open corridor, his arms flung **wide open**.

"We found Tulip!" Zoe said, pointing at me

sitting on the overturned bucket, wearing a beekeeper hat and gardening gloves.

"She's under the bucket," I explained.

Mr. Dougal's face lit up. "**Marvelous!**" he said. "Simply marvelous!"

"We came in here looking for her, and then the door shut and locked us in," Zoe explained. "We're not sure what to do now."

"You did exactly the right thing, although I imagine Tulip must be **very alarmed** with all the racket you were making!" He eyed the bucket underneath me. "Now the question is how we get Tulip out from under there, and back in her tank. I've got a **whole bag** of insects for her—she must be very hungry."

I gulped. I hoped she wasn't hungry enough to try to take a bite out of me!

"If we slide a piece of cardboard under the bucket, that should work," mused Mr. Dougal.

"How did Tulip escape in the first place?" I asked.

Mr. Dougal's cheeks turned red. "Instead of putting her back in her tank, like I should have done after showing her to your class, I set Tulip down on my desk. I've done it before, and **usually** she just sits there, much like a small contented cat, but this time she leaped off and ran into the hallway before anyone could

179

stop her!" He hurried on. "I'm ever so indebted to you all for finding her. I would have been **DEVASTATED** if she'd been lost for good! I must say, your methods are unusual, but clearly work." Understanding flashed across his face. "And I'm guessing you are responsible for the honey **all along** the halls?"

Zoe and I nodded. "We thought the honey could catch Tulip, or at least catch some flies to lure her."

Mr. Dougal stroked his chin and nodded. "That seems perfectly logical to me."

"Mr. Dougal," I said, "do you think you could try to move Tulip now? I've been sitting on this bucket for a long time."

"Oh, **of course!**" said Mr. Dougal. He looked around the supply closet and then grabbed a plastic folder. "This will work even better than cardboard."

I hopped off the bucket, and watched as Mr. Dougal deftly slid the plastic folder under the bucket, and then lifted them both up. I could see the shadow and shape of Tulip **scampering** around, but she didn't get out. "Come along, Tulip," Mr. Dougal sang. "Time to go home."

Zoe and I followed Mr. Dougal into the science lab, just to be sure that Tulip made it back into her tank. He slid her into the glass cage gently, and she immediately scuttled over to a **giant leaf**.

"Make sure to close the lid!" I said. I knew from experience that sometimes creatures get out of their enclosures when you least expect it.

"Thank you both for your help," said Mr. Dougal, smiling at us. He looked around. "Weren't there three of you?"

"Bernard didn't like being locked in the closet," I explained. "He's probably outside getting some **fresh air**."

"Very wise," said Mr. Dougal. "But as I was

saying, thank you—all of you—for your help. I'm very impressed by your bravery and creativity. Don't worry about the honey mess you made—I'll clean that up. And I'll write your teacher a note explaining why you are late for class, and that you **saved the day**. Hopefully she can give you some extra credit or something."

"That's okay," I said. "We didn't find Tulip for extra credit. We did it because we knew we were the only ones who could." And I felt braver than I ever had.

"Well, you can always come back and visit Tulip any time you like," said Mr. Dougal.

"I think we've probably seen **enough of Tulip** for now," said Zoe politely. "But thank you."

When we got back to class, Bernard was already there, standing at the front and telling everyone what had happened. Ms. Winkleworth looked slightly skeptical.

"*They* can tell you!" Bernard said, pointing at us.

I handed Ms Winkleworth the note from Mr. Dougal. "It's all true," I said. "We're **OFFICIAL SPIDER CATCHERS** now."

Everyone wanted to hear the details, and Ms Winkleworth let us tell the class all about it.

"**Weren't you scared?**" Zach asked. He's one of Ralph's friends and sometimes calls me Scaredy-Cat Sam, too, but this time it didn't sound like he was making fun of me.

I shook my head. I had been a *little* bit scared,

but I knew now that being brave sometimes means facing something even if it scares you.

"Who would have thought that Scaredy-Cat Sam would catch the spider?" said Ralph. He was kind of smiling and kind of smirking, but at least he wasn't snorting. I even thought I heard him mumble to himself that it was "kind of cool."

"It's **VERY** cool," said Regina. "I just wish I had been there when you caught Tulip in the bucket." Then she looked at me, Bernard, and Zoe. "I'll definitely be there when you catch our zombie werewolf, though!" At the mention of the zombie werewolf, Ralph went pale.

Just because I was now an official spider catcher didn't mean I was ready to face a **zombie werewolf!** But I smiled at Regina and said, "That will be no problem!"

Next to me, Bernard and Zoe groaned, but

they were smiling, too.

We'd faced our fear of spiders and proved to everyone that we were **NOT** afraid.

After school that day, I re-created the whole thing for Lucy. She was a great audience, gasping and cheering at all the right times.

"Do you want to come into my **spider court?**" she asked. "Now that you know about it, you can visit any time."

"No, thanks," I said. "I think I've seen enough spiders to last me a lifetime!"

"I know I wasn't with you when you caught Tulip, but can I be a member of the spider-catcher club, too?" Lucy said.

I grinned. "Of course. You're a very important member." Then I paused. "In fact, not only are you a member of the spider-catcher club, you're now officially a member of the **SPACE BLASTERS** crew, too. If you'd like to be, that is."

Lucy beamed.

"Definitely!" she said. Then her smile faltered. "Does this mean I have to watch **SPACE BLASTERS** with you all the time?"

I laughed. "Only when you want to."

"Okay, good," she said. "You watch a **LOT** of **SPACE BLASTERS**."

I shot my hand up in the air like a rocket, and Lucy did the same thing.

"For the universe!"

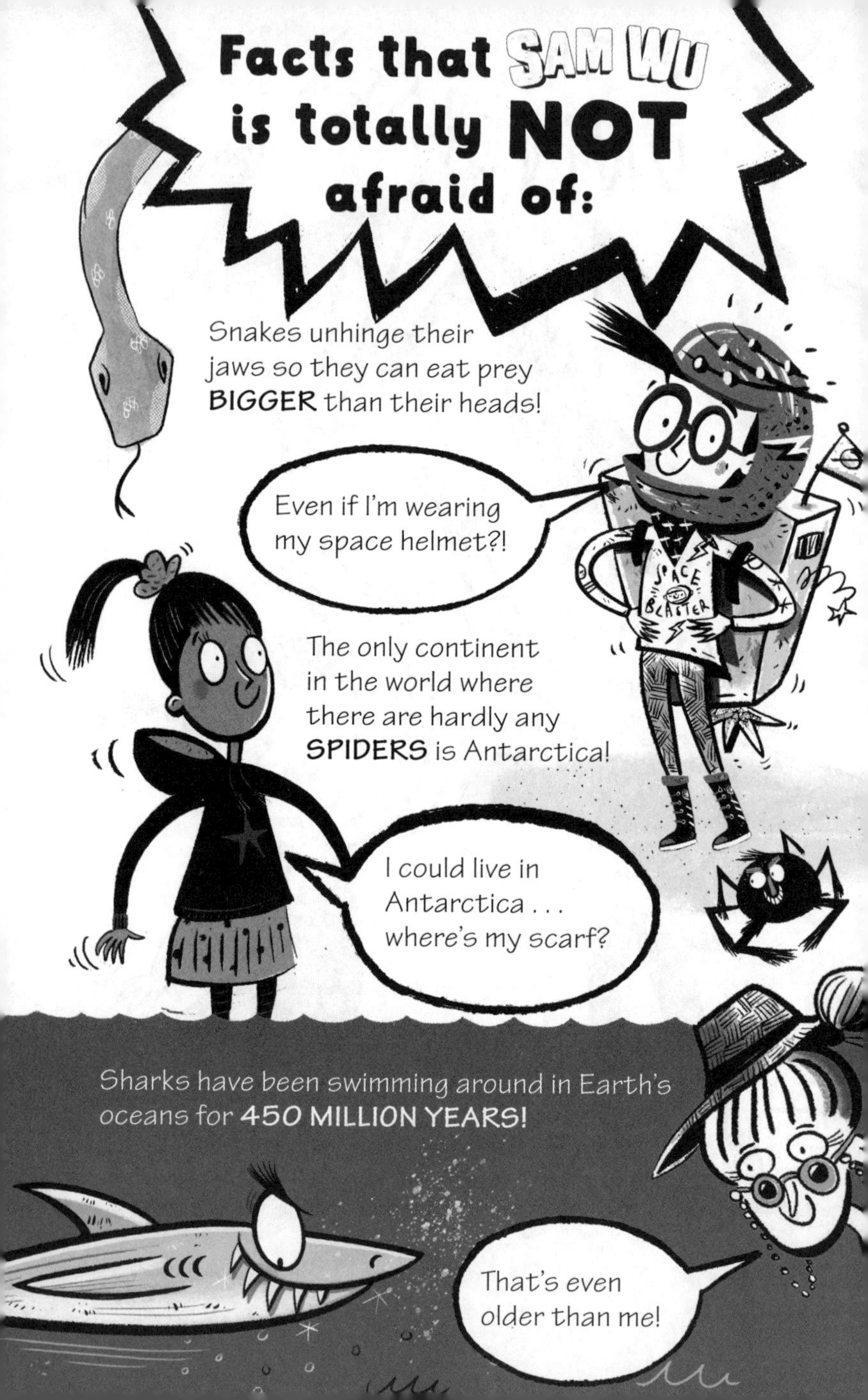

If you find the dark a little bit scary, you might want to consider turning into a small mammal called a Tarsier. **THEIR EYES ARE BIGGER THAN THEIR BRAINS,** and they can catch their small prey in complete darkness!

I think I'd rather have a big brain.

Footprints made by astronauts on the moon could stay there for **MILLIONS AND MILLIONS OF YEARS,** as there is no wind or water to wash them away.

That would not happen in the Wu household!

Bears do not pee during hibernation— that means they hold it in for **HALF A YEAR!**

I'm glad I'm a cat.

SAM WU IS NOT JOKING!
(Except that he is)

What do you get if you cross an alien with a tasty campfire treat?

A MARTIAN-MALLOW!

Why was Butterbutt the cat sitting on Lucy's computer keyboard?

To keep an eye on the mouse!

Why did Bernard run away from the tree?

Because he was afraid of the bark!

ACKNOWLEDGMENTS

We love writing Sam Wu—but we couldn't have made it into a real book that you can hold in your hands without the help and support of some amazing people!

If we had our own spaceship on *Space Blasters*, our captain would be Claire Wilson, our fearless agent who always guides us in the right direction. Thank you for believing in us and believing in Sam Wu.

We are tremendously grateful to everyone at our publisher, Sterling Books for supporting Sam Wu, especially our wonderful editor Rachael Stein and copyeditor Brian Phair. Thank you as well to our UK publisher, Egmont.

Huge thank-you to our incredibly talented illustrator, Nathan Reed, for bringing Sam and his friends to life on the page! The illustrations are our favorite part of the book and they somehow keep getting better and better! We are very lucky authors.

Thank you as well to our designer, Lizzie Gardiner at Egmont, who made the pages look so awesome. And thank you to the publicity, sales, and marketing teams for their support, especially Lauren Tambini.

We'd like to thank our families and friends for all their support and excitement. Special thank you to our grandparents, to whom this book is dedicated, our siblings, and our parents.

And to Baby Tsang, who will be in the world by the time this book comes out. We love you.

Turn the page to get a sneak peek at another of Sam's exciting adventures!

Sam Wu is absolutely, positively, definitely NOT afraid of ghosts. All he needs is a terrifying and deadly pet as a sidekick, and to defeat the Ghost King once and for all. Easy! Right . . . ?

STERLING CHILDREN'S BOOKS
New York

CHAPTER 1

DON'T CALL ME SCAREDY-CAT SAM

My name is **Sam Wu,** and I am <u>**NOT**</u> afraid of ghosts.

I know this for a fact because I recently had to become a genuine, certified[1] **ghost hunter**. Some people might try to tell you otherwise. But those people are **LIARS**. Do <u>**NOT**</u> listen to them. Especially do not listen to them if their name is **Ralph Philip Zinkerman the Third**. Ralph will tell you

---

[1] Certification came from my friend Zoe, but that's not important.

that I am . . . Scaredy-Cat Sam.

For the record, I am **<u>NOT</u>** a scaredy-cat.
If I were a cat, I'd be like my little sister
Lucy's cat, Butterbutt. **DO <u>NOT</u> BE
FOOLED BY THE NAME.**

Butterbutt is an

EVIL NINJA!

HI-YAA!

Even my Na-Na (that's my grandma — she lives with us) is **scared** of Butterbutt, and she is so brave that one time **she wrestled an ALLIGATOR!**

When I tried to explain to Ralph that:

A.   I am __NOT__ a scaredy-cat and

B.   Scaredy-Cat doesn't make sense as an insult

he just laughed at me and said I was probably scared of cats, too. **Which obviously ISN'T TRUE.**

He's never met Butterbutt. I bet **he'd** be scared of Butterbutt.

I mean, seriously! LOOK AT HIM!

You are probably wondering why Ralph calls me **Scaredy-Cat Sam**.

Now listen closely, because I'm only going to tell this story **ONCE**. Okay? I don't even let my best friends Zoe and Bernard talk about it. And we talk about **everything**. But even they know **NOT** to ever mention it. It isn't a laughing matter, no matter what some people might tell you.

It should have been the **best day of the year**. It was the day of the class field trip to the **Space Museum**. It was all I had thought about for months. You see, the Space Museum had a **REAL** spaceship in it. The only spaceship I'd ever seen was on my favorite TV show

I was **so excited**, I even wore my special spaceman gear, which was carefully crafted by

SPACE BLASTERS' **number one fan** (i.e. me).

Unfortunately, space gear is expensive.
So I had to be resourceful and make my own
even-better space equipment. All it took was

a bike helmet, some
plastic wrap, and a
few flashlights (**it's
dark in space**).
I even made a
custom
SPACE BLASTERS
shirt with some
felt tip markers.

I thought it
was going to be a
perfect day.

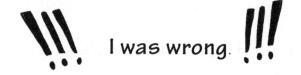

I was wrong.

It all started when I got on the bus to go to the museum. I sat down next to Zoe and Bernard, **proudly** wearing my SPACE BLASTERS T-shirt and specially crafted space helmet.

"Sam," said Bernard, blinking at me. **"What exactly are you wearing?"** He was holding a lightsaber and wearing a *Star Wars* T-shirt. A fancy one. <u>NOT</u> one that he had made himself.

"Yeah," said Zoe, frowning at my T-shirt. "What's a space blaster?"

This was <u>NOT</u> the reaction I was expecting.

"Oh," I said as I pointed at my T-shirt.

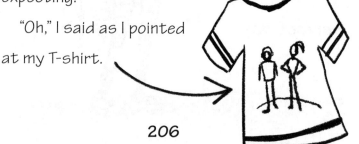

"This is Spaceman Jack, and this is Captain Jane!" Or at least it was supposed to be. **Drawing is <u>NOT</u> one of my talents.**

My friends stared at me blankly.

"Spaceman Jack and Captain Jane?" asked Bernard.

"Hmm . . . I should have drawn Five-Eyed Frank, huh? He's probably more recognizable."

"Five-Eyed Frank? What are you talking about?" asked Zoe.

I looked around the bus, and I realized that **NOBODY** had any kind of **SPACE BLASTERS** gear on. I didn't get it! **SPACE BLASTERS** is the

BEST SHOW IN THE UNIVERSE. And BEYOND!

"You know — **SPACE BLASTERS?**"

Their expressions told me that they did **NOT** know about **SPACE BLASTERS.**

"It's all about Captain Jane and Spaceman Jack's adventures with their alien friend Five-Eyed Frank. They travel on TUBS, which stands for 'The Universe's Best Spacecraft,' and **BLAST** through wormholes to other galaxies and fight bad guys. It's the **BEST!**"

"So . . . it's like a less cool *Star Wars?*" asked Bernard.

"No," I scoffed. "It's **WAY** cooler." I actually wasn't totally sure. I'd never seen *Star Wars.*

Zoe and Bernard were still looking at me

like they didn't believe **SPACE BLASTERS** was the best show in all of the universe. "You'll understand when you watch it," I said.

"All right," Zoe said, and Bernard nodded. And then we were at the Space Museum.

And that is when it all **REALLY** went wrong.

And don't miss Sam's other adventures!

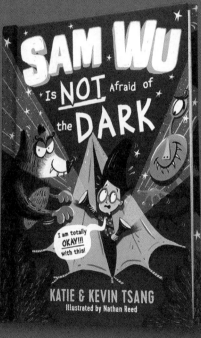

STERLING CHILDREN'S BOOKS
New York